ZACHARY
in
The Wawabongbong

by Bertrand Gauthier
illustrations by Daniel Sylvestre

Gareth Stevens Publishing
MILWAUKEE

For a free color catalog describing Gareth Stevens's list of high-quality books, call 1-800-341-3569 (USA) or 1-800-461-9120 (Canada).

Library of Congress Cataloging-in-Publication Data

ISBN 0-8368-1011-2

This edition first published in 1993 by
Gareth Stevens Publishing
1555 North RiverCenter Drive, Suite 201
Milwaukee, Wisconsin 53212, USA

This edition first published in 1993 by Gareth Stevens, Inc. Original edition
©1989 by Les éditions la courte échelle inc., Montréal, under the title *Zunik dans le wawazonzon*.

Series editor: Patricia Lantier-Sampon
Series designer: Karen Knutson

Printed in the United States of America
1 2 3 4 5 6 7 8 9 9 97 96 95 94 93

At this time, Gareth Stevens, Inc., does not use 100 percent recycled paper, although the paper used in our books does contain about 30 percent recycled fiber. This decision was made after a careful study of current recycling procedures revealed their dubious environmental benefits. We will continue to explore recycling options.

Today, my father and I are going to take the subway downtown to buy presents for Helen, Marlene, and Grandma. Then, we're going to visit the Land of the Wawabongbong.

We are not driving downtown this time. My father says it is easier and more fun to take the subway to go Christmas shopping.

Finally, we get there. There are already lots of people waiting at the Land of the Wawabongbong. We have to hurry up.

That's the way my father is. He always has plenty of time to talk to his friends. . .

. . .but never enough time for me.

Finally, I reach the entrance to the Land of
the Wawabongbong.

I never imagined the wawabongbong would be so big.

WHITE MOUNTAIN LIBRARY
Sweetwater County Library System
Rock Springs, Wyoming

PICTURE

10/93

WHITE MOUNTAIN LIBRARY
2935 SWEETWATER DRIVE
ROCK SPRINGS, WY   82901
362-2665

GAYLORD

Suddenly, I feel very small. I look
everywhere, but I can't see my father.

I might be. . . I think I am. . . I *know* I'm lost.

Whew, just in time! I was really scared.
I've never been so happy to see
my father.

I take his hand and hold it very tightly.
I do not want to lose him again.

I sure love my father when he worries about me.